Can You Say Peace?

Karen Katz

Henry Holt and Company

New York

Henry Holt and Company, LLC
Publishers since 1866
175 Fifth Avenue
New York, New York 10010
www.henryholtchildrensbooks.com

Library of Congress Cataloging-in-Publication Data
Katz, Karen.
Can you say peace? / Karen Katz.—1st ed.
p.   cm.
Summary: Every September 21 on the International Day of Peace,
children around the world wish in many different languages for peace.
ISBN-13: 978-0-8050-7893-0
ISBN-10: 0-8050-7893-2
[1. International Day of Peace—Fiction. 2. Peace—Fiction.] I. Title.
PZ7.K15745Can 2006   [E]—dc22   2005012857

First Edition—2006 / Designed by Laurent Linn
The artist used collage and mixed media to create the illustrations for this book.
Printed in the United States of America on acid-free paper. ∞

1 3 5 7 9 10 8 6 4 2

To all the children around the world,
our peacemakers of the future

Thanks to Kate Farrell, Laurent Linn, and Elaine Schiebel

Special thanks to Janos Tisovszky
and everyone at the United Nations
who taught me so many different ways
to say peace

Today is Peace Day
all around the world.
Children everywhere will
wish for peace,
hope for peace,
and ask for peace.

All around the world today,
there will be many
different ways to say
peace.

Meena lives in India.

Meena says *shanti* (SHAHN-tee).

Emily lives in America.

Emily says *peace*.

Kenji lives in Japan.

Kenji says *heiwa* (hey-wah).

Lynette lives in Australia.

Lynette says *kurtuku* (kur-TU-ku).

Carlos lives in Mexico.

Carlos says *paz* (pahs).

Hana lives in Iran.

Hana says *sohl* (sohl).

Stefan lives in Russia.

Stefan says *mir* (meer).

May lives in China.

May says *he ping* (hey ping).

Claire lives in France.

Claire says *paix* (pay).

Sadiki lives in Ghana.

Sadiki says *goom-jigi* (goom-jee-jee).

Alona lives in Bolivia.

Alona says *mojjsa kamaña* (moh-khsah ka-mah-neeah).

All around the world, children want
to go to school,

to walk in their towns and cities,

to play outside,

and to share food with their families.

They want to do all these things and feel safe.
No matter how we say it, we all want peace.

Can you say peace?

shanti   paix   he ping

mir